When Night Time Comes Near

Judy Pedersen

VIKING

VIKING

Published by the Penguin Group

Penguin Putnam Books for Young Readers,

345 Hudson Street, New York, New York 10014, U.S.A.

Penguin Books Ltd, Registered Offices:

Harmondsworth, Middlesex, England

First published in 2000 by Viking,

a division of Penguin Putnam Books for Young Readers.

10 9 8 7 6 5 4 3 2 1

LIBRARY OF CONGRESS CATALOGING-IN-PUBLICATION DATA

Pedersen, Judy.

When night time comes near / by Judy Pedersen.   p. cm.

Summary: A child describes what happens as day turns to night and bedtime approaches.

ISBN 0-670-88259-3

[1. Night—Fiction. 2. Bedtime—Fiction.] I. Title.

PZ7.P34235Wh 2000 [E]—dc21 98-44366 CIP AC

Printed in Hong Kong   Set in Bodoni

For Elia,
Briana,
and Mabel

When night time comes near
and your house turns to gold
and the cat begins to *meeeow*,
it's time to go in.

Mr. Mann folds his flag and
turns on his porch light.

Miss Isabel and her sister Tilly collect lawn chairs
and croquet balls to put them away.

The lamp is lit in the window
so Mother and Father can read
their books as the sun goes down.

When night time comes near
and the breeze goes to sleep,
you can see the sun slide behind
the hills and the stars shimmer
like clean pennies.

Salamanders wiggle their smooth bodies under the leaves. They are looking for a dark resting place.

The lilies close their petals tightly.
Tomorrow they will open again with the light.

Squirrels are tired
from collecting acorns.
Scampering up the trees,
they settle in their
nests and fall asleep.

Now night time is here.

Good night Miss Isabel and Tilly.
Good night lilies and salamanders.

Good night Mr. Mann and sleepy squirrels.

Good night sun.

Hello moon.

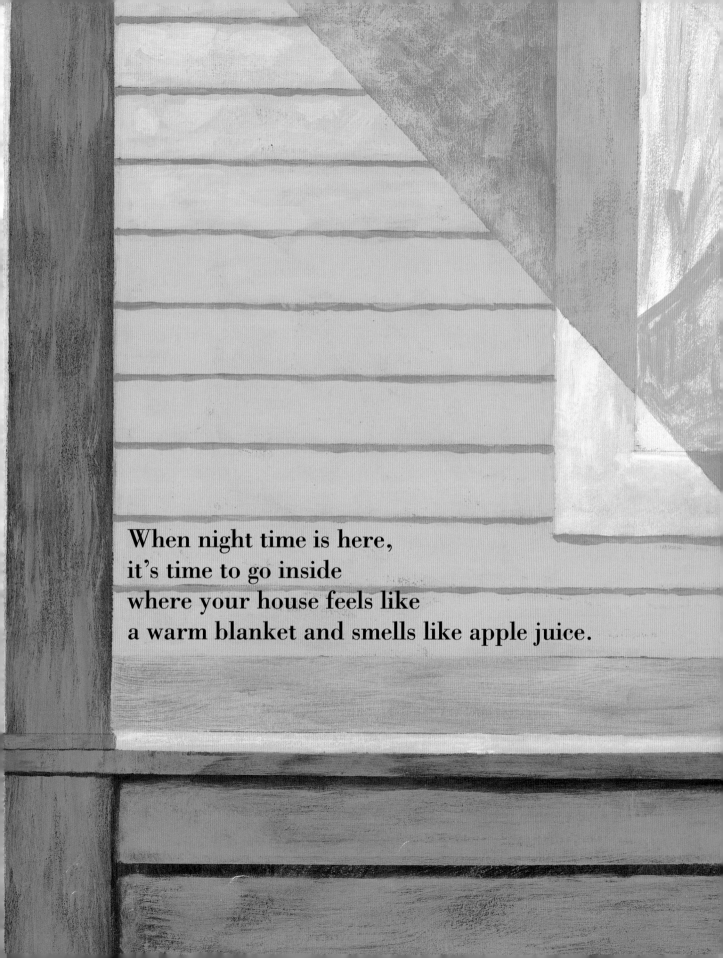

When night time is here,
it's time to go inside
where your house feels like
a warm blanket and smells like apple juice.

It's time to take off your jacket and cap and brush the leaves from your hair.

It's time to wash your face
and hands and brush
your teeth, too.

'Night Mother and Father.

'Night little brown cat.

For when night time is here
and you hear the
climbing roses whisper,
you will be dreaming.